E
PE

Peet, Bill

No such things

DATE DUE			
MY 9 '89	JY 16 '90	OC 4 '93	
MY 26 '89	AG 25 '90	JAN 3 '90	JUL 15 '9
	AG 29 '90	AUG 11 '9	AUG 13 '98
AG 21 '88	SE 24 '90	AUG 15 '94	OCT 22 '98
NO 11 '89	JA 23	NOV 30 '94	NOV 18 '98
NO 20	FE 22	JUN 05 '9	DEC 15 '98
DE 26 '89	SE 11 '90	NOV 6 '95	
JA 13 '90	AG 31 '92	JUL 25 '96	22
FE 5 '90	NO 13 '92	JUL 22 '97	AP 19 '99
		SEP 22	
MR 17 '90	FE 13 '93	FEB 17	MY 21 '99
AP 21 '90	MR 4 '93	APR 06 '98	JY 07 '99
MY 16 '90	SE 7 '93	JUN 16 '98	NO 26 '99

JA 03 '00
MR 04 '00

© THE BAKER & TAYLOR CO.

NO SUCH THINGS

HOUGHTON MIFFLIN COMPANY   BOSTON   1983

Bill Peet

Library of Congress Cataloging in Publication Data

Peet, Bill.
  No such things.

  Summary: Describes in rhyme a variety of fantastical
creatures such as the blue-snouted Twumps, the pie-faced
Pazeeks, and the fancy Fandangos.
  [1. Stories in rhyme. 2. Animals, Mythical—Fiction.
3. Humorous stories] I. Title.
PZ8.3.P2764No 1983   [E]   82-23234
ISBN 0-395-33888-3

Printed in the United States of America
  H10 9 8 7 6 5 4 3 2 1

To my
brand-new grandson
MICHAEL

The blue-snouted Twumps feed entirely on weeds,
And along with the weeds they swallow the seeds.
Eating seeds causes weeds to sprout on their backs,
Till they look very much like walking haystacks.
When a mother Twump has young ones to raise,
Her weed-covered back is where they all graze.
Of all the odd creatures, you won't find another
Who supports its young as both fodder and mother.

The Glubzunks, who resemble big old sunken logs,
Keep a hungry eye out for plump juicy frogs.
Since old sunken logs are where frogs like to hide,
When they spy a Glubzunk they go swimming inside.

But Glubzunks are slow witted and not at all clever,
And to shut their big mouths takes them almost forever.
By then all the frogs, I am happy to say,
Have made their escape and are swimming away.

The golden brown crested, pie-faced Pazeeks
Have huge appetites to match their big beaks.
And their three-toed, unusual, pitchfork-like feet
Are perfect for picking the cherries they eat.

To make sure everyone in the flock gets his share,
There's a strict pecking order to keep it all fair.
This means that the smaller ones stay in their places
Till the bigger Pazeeks are done filling their faces.

The common big wig-tailed Mopwoggins
Have no hair at all on their noggins.
That's the main reason why they're so sheepish and shy,
And also the reason they are crafty and sly.

They hide their bare heads in a very strange way,
By using their tails as a perfect toupee.
And no one would guess that their noggins were hairless,
If the sheepish Mopwoggins were not sometimes careless.

It's no fun for the Flumpers to crawl on the ground,
So they coil themselves up to be perfectly round.
Then they go for a spin, a wild whirling ride,
Far out in the hilly, broad countryside.

After so many miles of rolling about,
They discover their rubbery hides have worn out.
Since they can't be retreaded once they go flat,
There's nothing the Flumpers can do after that.

13

The Juggarums have a most impolite way
Of overpowering their high-flying, lacy-winged prey.
They use their strong breath, one potent *ker-puff*,
To stun dragonflies if they fly close enough.

Then the dragonflies drop as if someone had shot them,
With no idea of just what could have got them.
Then cross-eyed and dizzy, down the flies come,
To end up inside of the old Juggarum.

The spooky-tailed Tizzy has a brain that's so small,
She forgets everything in just no time at all.
That is why her own tail is a shocking surprise,
With its ferocious jaws and enormous red eyes.

16

One glimpse of the thing and she lets out a shriek,
Flies into a Tizzy, takes off like a streak.
She runs on for miles just screaming in terror,
Before she discovers her horrible error.

17

The reason the Flubduds all sigh in despair —
They stand on their feet and can't go anywhere.
Since they're much too befuddled to figure things out,
They're stuck in one spot and can't move about.

It always will be quite a while between feasts,
For these awkward, dim-witted, grass-eating beasts.
And they won't get one nibble, not one bite to eat,
Till the prairie grass grows almost up to their feet.

The great Gullagaloops with their yawning fish faces
Live deep in the sea in the gloomiest places.
And since they're so long and completely strung out,
They lose track of themselves while they're swimming about.

When they catch a sardine, more often than not
It turns out to be their own tail that they've got.
So they don't dare to trust or believe their own eyes,
For fear they might catch themselves by surprise.

If the fancy Fandangos seem stuck-up and snooty,
It is mostly because of their exquisite beauty.
They're most often seen with smug smiling faces,
By a crystal clear pond in a jungle oasis.

There they linger for hours with nothing to do
But sip the sweet water and admire the view.
And the view they admire, as you might well suppose,
Is their own reflection, right under their nose.

23

The Grabnabbits are an odd undersea growth —
Not plants nor animals, but mixtures of both.
These creatures catch fish but they never eat one —
They do not have gullets, so they catch them for fun.

To them a codfish is just something to tease,
To grab by the tail, to pinch, or to squeeze.
But the poor frightened fish cannot possibly know
That they will not be eaten — until they're let go.

The sly, snickering Snoof lives up where it snows,
So he always leaves tracks wherever he goes.
When he runs to the west, this wrong-way-footed beast
Leaves a trail of huge bear tracks that seem to go east.

When hunters discover the trail of the brute,
They suppose it's a bear and get ready to shoot.
They never suspect that they've been led astray
By a creature whose feet go the opposite way.

The pin-headed Magawk who towers up to the sky
Has a bird's-eye view even though he can't fly.
And since his beak is so amazingly small,
He must feed on the tiniest creatures that crawl.

And with so much frenzied pecking to do,
He sees things more often from a worm's-eye view.
With his beak an inch or two from the ground,
He peeks into crannies where bugs can be found.

The Skeezaboos' skis are completely self-grown,
So you might say these skiers ski on their own.
Ker-swoosh! They take off in a smooth, easy glide,
Aboard their big horns down a steep mountainside.

The Skeezaboos could have a wonderful time
If the return trip weren't such a torturous climb.
When the horns hook on snags and keep bumping their knees,
Then they wish they weren't quite so attached to their skis.

When the Flumox goes fishing he doesn't need bait,
All he needs is the patience to sit still and wait.
First he picks out a spot where it's shady and cool,
And he lets his long beard flow down into a pool.
Then deep in his gullet the foxy old Flumox
Makes a sound just like water running over the rocks.
Soon the fish come leaping up the fake waterfall,
Then *glug-aloop!*—the sly Flumox swallows them all.